I'm Glad I'm Your
GRANDMA

written by Bill and Kathy Horlacher

illustrated by Kathryn Hutton

Third Printing, 1989

Library of Congress Catalog Card No. 86-63568
©1987. The STANDARD PUBLISHING Company, Cincinnati, Ohio
Division of STANDEX INTERNATIONAL Corporation. Printed in U.S.A.

I'm glad I'm your grandma!
Please let me say why . . .

I'm glad I'm your grandma
when we go for a walk—

or sit on the porch
just to have a nice talk.

I'm glad I'm your grandma
when you send me a card—

or you draw me a picture,
which shows you've tried hard.

I'm glad I'm your grandma
when you call on the phone—

or you come for a visit
just to see me at home.

I'm glad I'm your grandma
when we ride in the car—

or when it's all dark,
and we see a bright star.

I'm glad I'm your grandma
when you give me a squeeze—

or you ask for a favor,
and politely say "please."

I'm glad I'm your grandma
when we go to the park—

and we play on the swings
until it gets dark.

I'm glad I'm your grandma
when you kiss me good-night—

or you ask for a hug
when things aren't quite right.

I'm glad I'm your grandma
when we take time to play—

and when talking to God
you have plenty to say.

I'm glad I'm your grandma
when we share something sweet—

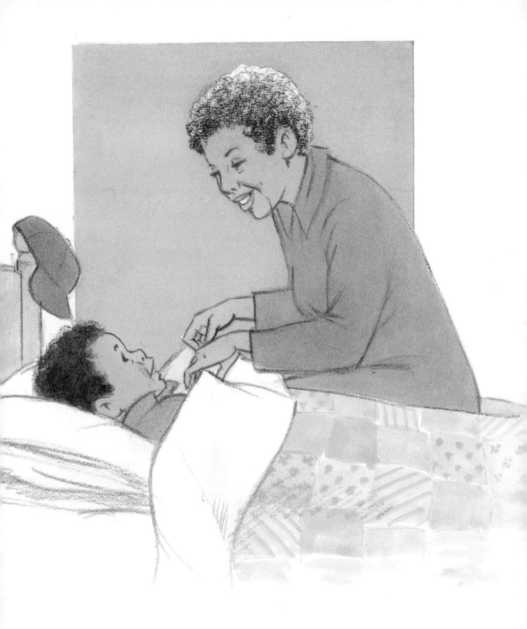

or I tuck you in tight,
and then sing you to sleep.

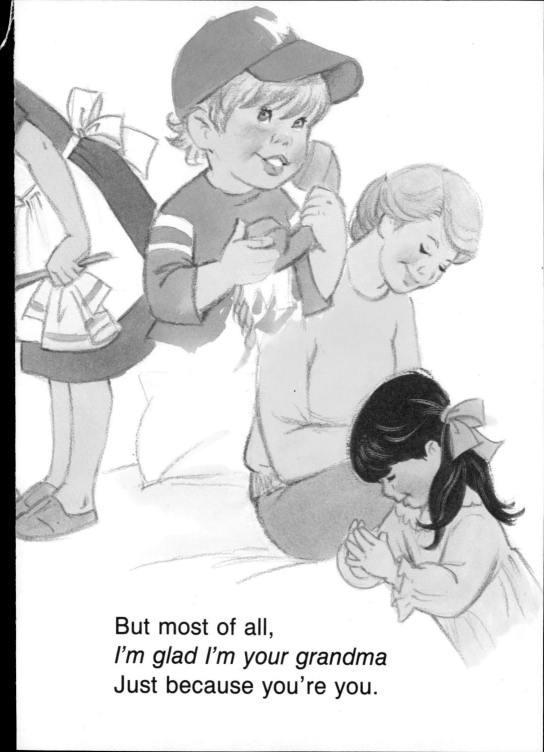

But most of all,
I'm glad I'm your grandma
Just because you're you.

You're God's wonderful gift to me!